This Little Tiger book belongs to:

_____

_____

_____

The Teeny Weeny

For Veronica and Rye Mepham
at the Rescuers Wildlife Sanctuary – S C

For Ethan – J T

LITTLE TIGER PRESS
1 The Coda Centre, 189 Munster Road, London SW6 6AW
www.littletiger.co.uk

First published in Great Britain 2005
This edition published 2016

Based on the title LOOK OUT FOR THE BIG BAD FISH!
by Sheridan Cain and Tanya Linch

A CIP catalogue record for this book is available from the British Library

Tadpole

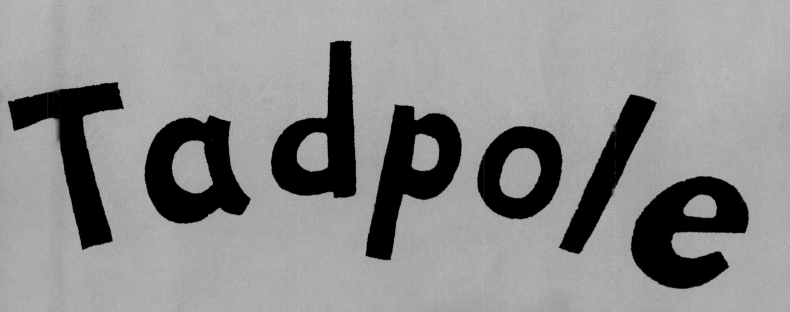

Sheridan Cain

Jack Tickle

LITTLE TIGER PRESS
London

The teeny weeny tadpole
swam in and out of the lily pads.
Splish! Splash!
  "Hello, my busy little tadpole,"
said Mother Frog. "It's a lovely
day for splashing! And leaping . . ."

Boing!

Boing!
went Mother Frog,
high into the air.

Flippity-flop

Flippity-flop, she landed with
a plop!
  "I could do that," said Tadpole
and he tried to leap on to
the lily pad. All he managed
was a splish and a splash.

"Mum, why can't
I jump like you?"
asked Tadpole.
  "Oh but you will,
Tadpole," said
Mother Frog.
"You will. Just
keep splishing
and splashing!"

Tadpole swam off
downstream.
"Take care, Tadpole!"
called Mother Frog.
"Look out for the
big bad fish."

Tadpole wiggled his way to the
edge of the stream to splash among
the flowers. He looked up and saw
a woolly face with a smudgy nose.

"Hello," said Tadpole. "Who are you?"

"I'm Lamb," said the woolly-faced
creature.

"Can you jump?" asked Tadpole.

"You bet!" said Lamb. "Watch this!"

Boing!

Boing!
went Lamb,
high into the air.

Springity-sprong

Springity-sprong,
he landed with a bong!
 "Ooh!" said Tadpole. "I wish
I could jump like that."
 "Oh but you will, Tadpole," said
Lamb. "Soon, you will."

A few days later, Tadpole paddled downstream to where the violets tickled his tummy. He looked up and saw a twitchy nose and the largest pair of ears he'd ever seen.

"Hello," said Tadpole. "Who are you?"

"I'm Rabbit," said the twitchy-nosed creature.

"Can you jump?" asked Tadpole.

"Can I jump?" said Rabbit.
"Watch this!"

Boing!

Boing!
went Rabbit,
high into the air.

Jumpity-bump

Jumpity-bump, he landed
with a thump!
"Oh my," said Tadpole. "I wish
I could jump like that."
"Oh but you will, Tadpole,"
said Rabbit. "Very soon,
you will."

Several days later, Tadpole swam out to where the giant bulrushes wobbled in the wind. He saw a pair of bug eyes and two springy legs.

"Hello," said Tadpole. "Who are you?"

"I'm Grasshopper," said the bug-eyed creature.

"Can you jump?" asked Tadpole.

"Of course," said Grasshopper.
"Watch this!"

Boing!

Boing!
went Grasshopper,
high into the air.

Hippity-hop

Hippity-hop, he landed with
a bop!
  "Wow!" said Tadpole. "I wish
I could jump like that."
  "Oh but you will, Tadpole,"
said Grasshopper. "Very, very
soon, you will."

The next time Tadpole went exploring, he swam far out to where the stream widened and the water became clear. Tadpole looked down and saw a pair of huge, rubbery lips.

"Hello," said Tadpole. "Who are you?"
"Hello!" boomed the rubbery-lipped
creature. "I'm Big Bad Fish, and . . .

I eat tadpoles!"

The big bad
fish chased
Tadpole up . . .

and down . . .

and in
and out
of weeds . . .

getting
closer
and
closer
until . . .

Boing!

Tadpole leapt high into the air — higher than Lamb, higher than Rabbit and higher than Grasshopper. He leapt all the way home.

"Look, Mum!" said Tadpole.
"I can jump. Just like you!"
  His mother smiled proudly.
"Of course you can,
  my little FROG!"

CD track 1 – complete story with original music and sound effects
CD track 2 – story with page turn pings encourages learner readers to join in

Running time – over 15 mins • Produced by The Complete Works, Warwickshire CV31 1JP,
in conjunction with Stationhouse • Music composed by Jim Betteridge and Sam Park

Visit our website www.littletiger.co.uk for details of other Little Tiger Picture Book
and CD Sets, plus our full catalogue of novelty, board and picture books.